MAGNET

MASTER

TAYLER LOGUE

Independently Published

Copyright © 2021 by Tayler Logue

All rights reserved. No part of this book may be reproduced or used in any manner without written permission of the copyright owner except for the use of quotations in a book review.

This is a work of fiction. Names, characters, places, and incidents either are the product of the author's imagination or, if real, are used fictitiously.

First paperback edition 2021

ISBN: 978-0-578-93287-3

Cover Design by Basia Tran

To all my students

PROLOGUE

Hi! It's me, Koen. Hang on . . . you don't know who I am? I'd like to say, as politely as I can . . . how could you not?! Maybe you've heard of my superhero name, Magnet Master?

Nothing? Alright, I guess I'm going to have to start from the beginning to catch you up.

Don't worry, you're definitely going to enjoy my story. It has mystery, danger, suspense, heroics—and that's not just from my tricks on the monkey bars. But remember this is my actual life, so please don't laugh too hard at the embarrassing moments (because they were really, really embarrassing).

It began in science class. Fourth-grade science class to be exact. And science . . . well . . . let's just say it's not my favorite subject. *School* is not my favorite subject. I do not do well with any part of it, except recess. I CRUSH recess!

You really should see me on the monkey bars. They should rename them Koen bars.

Anyway, let me take you back to the beginning before I became Magnet Master.

CHAPTER 1

It is a dark and stormy night. Just kidding! This is not that kind of story. To tell the truth, it is a regular Wednesday.

I am sitting in science class, learning about . . . uh . . . let me think. Nope. I can't remember what we are learning about. Give it a moment, I'm sure my teacher Ms. L will say something soon.

Wait for it. Wait for it . . . Huh. Maybe she *won't* say anything. That's weird. It's literally her *job* to talk to us. I thought she would have said something by—

"Today your 'I can' statement is, 'I can discuss what happens to magnets when I put their poles together.'"

Oh yeah. There it is. I knew she'd say something. And now you know that we are learning about magnets and poles. Not the North Pole.

Ms. L shot down my idea of learning about polar bears. Apparently, *these* poles are on our magnets. I don't know if I believe that. I spent all class period yesterday looking for them and didn't even see one.

I glance around the room to see if the other students have finished writing their "I can" statements. Most of them have. They start to gather the science supplies. I rush up to the front to grab some too, but none are left.

"Ms. L, there aren't any more magnets!"

"Oh, I thought I had enough." Ms. L reaches into her desk drawer and pulls out two faded magnets. "Here you go!" she says cheerfully.

My classmates start to experiment with their magnets. Some are holding two magnets a little way apart. Once they let go, the magnets snap together making a *zzzz* sound.

Another group uses one magnet to push the other magnet away. But get this: it's not touching the magnet it's pushing away! *How does that happen?*

Ms. L keeps talking as she walks around the room. "I'm noticing that some of you are already figuring out the two ends of the magnets are different. Each end is called a 'pole.' The north pole is the negative end, painted red. The south pole is the positive end, painted black. When you put two positive ends together what happens?"

I have no clue what that means. I'm sure Ms. L will tell us in a few minutes anyway. The magnets look so fun to play with.

I grab them and start experimenting. That's right, I am now an experimenter. A scientist. The worst scientist in the history of scientists, but still a scientist.

I look across the table and see Emily, my best friend and science partner, digging through her pencil bag. She's probably lost her pencil. She does that a lot.

We became best friends last year because we were always late for school. We waited on the office bench together for the secretary to walk us to class. We were late *a lot.*

The secretary never found out why Emily was late. She would whisper the reason to me though. Most of the time it was because she lost her homework, water bottle, or socks around the house.

Emily doesn't talk much in school, especially when adults are around, but I talk. More than I should. The secretary always knew why I was late . . . I like to sleep in!

"Hey, Emily, what do you think will happen if we put this side of the magnet near the other magnet?" She shrugs her shoulders. "Alright, let's try it," I say, very determined.

She pushes one magnet closer to me. I hold mine a pencil length away and . . . nothing happens. We move our magnets closer until they are almost touching.

An invisible force pulls them out of our hands, and they snap together, making that *zzzz* sound! When the sound stops, the red and black parts are touching.

"That almost pinched my finger!" I shout.

Ms. L gives me a look that I know too well. It means to quiet down. I go back to working with Emily.

"What if we tried it the other way?"

We flip both magnets around and guess what?! They still snap together. *Hmmmm, how did Cabela and Kitana get theirs to push away?* I think to myself.

"Emily, only flip yours, okay?"

We bring both red parts (I think Ms. L called them north poles) closer together. We can't get them to *zzzz*.

Emily grabs both magnets and shoves them together. She squeezes. When she lets go, both magnets fly away. They slide in opposite directions across our desks, shooting onto the floor.

No, no, no!! I cannot lose these magnets! I am already in trouble with Ms. L for gluing my hand to the desk during our "Build a City" project.

I dive under the desk to find them. I immediately see one sticking to the leg of our table. I start to crawl across the floor looking for the other one.

I finally see it under the front table where Ms. L has her gigantic red horseshoe magnet with the silver ends. It doesn't seem fair that she has the biggest magnet I have ever seen. *Isn't the school on a budget?*

I crawl under Ms. L's table with one of the magnets in my hand, grab the other magnet, and pull myself up using the table. I should say, I *try* to pull myself up using the table. As I stand, it topples over. Maybe the school *is* on a budget . . . As the table falls, I also fall back down. The enormous magnet hits me in the back and lands beside me.

"Are you okay?" Ms. L asks as she rushes over.

I reach for the huge magnet to give it to Ms. L, and my hand slams against her magnet like I've lost control of it.

I try to yank it away, but my hand does not move. I'm stuck! I reach with my left hand to pull Ms. L's unnecessarily large magnet off my right hand.

A force pushes my hand toward the other side of the massive magnet, and then throws my hand back. My hand twists in the air.

THUNG!

The back of my hand gets trapped. *What?!* I see I am still holding the small magnets in the palms of my hands. I try pulling my hands off, but they will not budge. Now both my hands are trapped against the same side of this ridiculously GIGANTIC magnet!

In one final effort to remove my hands, I put my foot on the ENORMOUS magnet and push with all my might. *Pinch.* Suddenly, my hands fall away!

CHAPTER 2

Ms. L kneels. "Are you okay?"

I barely hear her. I stare at my hands. Hardcore staring. *Where did the magnets go? What happened?* I flip my hands over. And back over. Then back over again.

"Are you alright?"

As I inspect my hands, I notice red splotches have formed on the inside of both my palms where the small magnets used to be.

I snap back to reality as Ms. L grabs the large magnet and puts it, and the table, back in place. I realize that I am sprawled across the floor staring hard at my hands in front of the whole class.

I hear someone snickering and see Isaac quickly cover his mouth with his hand. I glare at him.

Mom says I shouldn't use the word hate, but I think there is no better way to describe my feelings toward him. I think he feels the same way. If we were in a superhero movie, I would be the hero of course. And Isaac . . . I'm sure you can already guess.

We have been sworn enemies from birth. We were destined to find each other to destroy everything and everyone the other cared about . . . Just kidding! Maybe Isaac isn't exactly a supervillain, but it would be cool to have a superhero back story.

The truth is Isaac and I used to be best friends, but we became enemies last summer. We would race each other on the monkey bars and teach each other cool tricks.

I started inviting Emily over to judge our tricks. For some reason, Isaac turned into a different person. A mean one. He started telling me that I was terrible at the monkey bars and acting like he was the best. His favorite phrase was, "You'll never be as good as me."

One day, I slipped during a trick and landed on my side. Isaac laughed and said, "You call that skill?" Then he turned to Emily, "What else can he mess up that badly? Nothing! I am so much better than that."

He didn't even care that I was hurt. After that, I stopped inviting him over.

"Koen, are you sure you're okay?" Ms. L is kneeling on the floor, eyebrows raised, waiting for me to respond.

Uh... "Yeah, I think I'm fine," I say.

I stand up and walk back to my desk. That was so weird.

"Where did our magnets go?" Emily asks.

I glance around the room again. "I have no clue."

Emily peaks under the desk. "I can't believe we lost them," she whispers, "That's the fourth thing today . . . my pencil, headband, spoon, and now the magnets..."

I pat her arm. Hopefully, Ms. L doesn't notice. I don't need another embarrassing "glued to desk" situation.

Ms. L tells us that it's time to put our magnets away and line up for recess. *Yes! Recess!!* I shrug at Emily, and we rush to line up.

CHAPTER 3

When we get outside, I run straight to the monkey bars. In case you hadn't noticed already, I'm a BOSS when it comes to tricks on the monkey bars.

But like all good things in life, I have to wait my turn. It's just like the movies, roller coasters, the diving board, fast food, and the water fountain after gym class.

There is a long line. So, I do what I always do in this situation. I yell at Isaac to "MOVE FASTER!!!!" Just joking; I'm too nice for that. But he's not.

"Haha! I guess you're just too slow, Koen. I'll always beat you. In a race, foursquare, or with any trick on the monkey bars," Isaac brags.

"Yeah, we'll see about that."

Isaac takes *forever* as he jumps to the fourth rung, turns around, and flips down. I try to keep myself from smiling. Is that the best he's got? Pretty basic stuff. Wait until I show him how it's done!

After *even more* waiting, it is *finally* my turn. I start with a side glare at Isaac. Then I prepare myself and others around me for my first trick.

I take a running leap through the air and aim for the last rung of the monkey bars. *This will show him!*

THUNG! My hands grab hold. I swing forward. I swing backward and prepare to twist myself around to land facing where I started.

I let go of the bar . . . At least, I *attempt* to let go of the bar, but my hands don't listen.

My body is yanked back. *AHHH!* My arms shout at me. *What in the world?* I stare up. My hands are still holding onto the monkey bars. *Why???*

I relax my grip again, but I don't fall. I am stuck, hanging from the monkey bars by my hands! In fact, my fingers are not even wrapped around the rung anymore. Just my palms are glued to it, but I swear I didn't touch any glue today!

I do what I imagine anyone in this situation would do. I handle myself with dignity and calm serenity.

No, I don't! I am LITERALLY STUCK TO THE MONKEY BARS!!!! I am a full-on spasming squirrel.

I turn my body every which way. I try pulling one arm off at a time, kicking my legs, pulling myself up, then dropping my body down. *AHHHHHHHHHH!*

I cannot even begin to tell you how much that last one hurt. But try to imagine.

On top of my physical agony, my classmates start yelling at me to get down so they can have a turn. Eli comes up to me and starts pulling on my leg. That bright idea leads to more people trying to tug me down. Even with five others attempting to free me, I still cannot let go!

I start to think we will bend the monkey bar. Or, more realistically, and much worse, my arms are going to be *RIPPED FROM MY BODY!!*

"Wow, you really showed me," Isaac laughs. "I don't think I've ever seen a trick that stupid before. Hanging from the monkey bars and pretending you can't let go . . . *very* original. I hate to say it, because all your tricks are awful, but even this summer you had better tricks than that. What happened? Haha!"

By now, the commotion caught Ms. L's attention. I see her start to fast walk in my direction. Her eyes meet mine with that questioning look, "Are you alright?"

I don't bother to respond. I am too busy trying to get down and shake these fools off me.

"Everyone needs to leave right now except for Koen."

The other students scatter. They find other games to join while still watching *The Koen Show*.

And me, I'm *still* hanging from the monkey bars. Ms. L waits until the students have cleared. She turns to me and puts her hand on a rung as she leans forward.

"Koen, why don't you drop down so we can talk about what happened?"

"I can't get down."

She smiles at me. "Have you tried letting go?"

"But I—"

"Can," she finishes for me.

I see that this is going about as well as it did with my classmates. Usually, she is super understanding.

"Think about it. Then try to let go," she says.

And for the record, I *am* trying. I look up at my hands, uncurl my fingers from the bar, and concentrate like my life depends on it. *Please let go. Please let me drop.*

I feel a pinch in my hands. *Oww!* My hands fly away from the bars, and I drop.

"This is a miracle! I'm free!!"

"Whatever you say," Ms. L chuckles.

As I walk in from recess, I look down at my hands. There is no longer a red splotch on the inside of my hands. In the center of my palms, there is a black bruise.

CHAPTER 4

For my own mental and physical safety (I'm looking at you Eli), I try not to touch anything throughout the rest of the day.

I don't want any more embarrassing moments. I don't think I could make it through elementary school and will NOT make it through middle school if my image takes another hit.

I'm already the class screwup. Getting stuck to the monkey bars, losing my magnets, gluing my hand to my desk, getting stuck in a tree at recess for hours . . .

Climbing down the firetruck's ladder was awesome, but also super embarrassing. And all that is only from this week!

Most of the kids in my class just laugh at me when that stuff happens. I laughed along with them at first, but after a while, it made me sad. I realized the only reason other kids want to hang out with me is to see what silly thing will happen to me next.

Emily is different. She doesn't care that I end up in embarrassing situations, and most of the time she tries to help me find a way out of it. Maybe it's because we became friends last year.

Actually, that can't be it. I had a lot of embarrassing moments then too. But I will not have more embarrassing moments today! I will NOT. TOUCH. ANYTHING.

Not touching anything is much harder than it sounds. Chair, desk, pencil, pencil bag, notebook, planner, drinking fountain, toilet flushing lever, locker, backpack, shoelaces, doors. When I can, I use my feet, wrists, or elbows. I will NOT touch anything with the palms of my hands.

At the end of the day, I almost forget and reach for the door. At the last second, I pull back and feel a pinch. *That was close!*

Besides that one close call, I crushed it. I mean, kicking open the doors at the end of the school day made me look like a BOSS; even though, Ms. L didn't agree. Also, I found a great new way to flush toilets.

I get home and run through the door as my mom holds it open. I drop my backpack at the edge of the counter and run to the fridge. I grab the fridge and whip it open looking for the yogurt my mom said she bought.

"Remember to eat some veggies first!" Mom shouts down the hall after me.

I make a *yuck* face and choose to ignore that comment. Mom knows how much I hate vegetables.

Aha! I found them. I reach for a yogurt but instead smash my hand into a closed fridge . . . and I'm stuck. Not this again!

I use my free hand to grab the freezer door to use as leverage to pull my hand off the fridge door. And now that one is stuck too! *UUGH!*

I can't believe I'm stuck to the fridge like a magnet!! Try as I might, my hands will not budge. I sink to the floor, and my hands slide down the fridge door.

Wait . . . I can move them! YES! I start to shimmy my hands down the fridge until I reach the edge. One, two, three! I yank my hands straight down.

"I'm free!"

I'm free, but with no yogurt. I stare down the fridge as if it is my mortal enemy. How can I get to the yogurt? If I touch the fridge, my hands will stick to it. Then it hits me: I should use my feet!

They didn't stick to the door I kicked open at school, so they shouldn't stick here. I swing my foot up and catch it in the handle. I bend my knee, pulling my leg into my body. I grunt as the suction gives way, and the fridge door swings open. VICTORY!

"What are you doing?"

I whip around to see my mom looking at me. I try to picture what she saw: me jumping up and down on one foot in front of the open fridge with my other leg in the door. Yeah, I don't know how to explain this one.

So, I answer, "What anyone in my position would do."

"Ah, yes. A true ninja in training," Mom laughs.

I snatch my yogurt and run downstairs making sure to kick the fridge shut behind me. I don't need to be trapped on the fridge like a refrigerator magnet.

Our fridge is full of cat magnets. Apparently, magnets with kittens hanging from a tree remind Mom to "Hang in There." I don't see why she needs that motivation. I'm a delight to have around.

As I enjoy the deliciousness that is yogurt, I start to think about what I am going to do. *What if I keep getting stuck to things? How do I make it stop?*

So far, I have been stuck to Ms. L's magnet, the monkey bars, and the fridge. I was able to slide my hands off the fridge, but not on the monkey bars or the magnet. And something happened with my hands when I thought really hard about letting go.

I look down at my hands. My palms are red again. I thought it was black earlier . . .? I close my eyes. I remember the moment I let go of the monkey bars, how badly I wanted to let go.

Ow! I feel a pinch in my hands again. My eyes widen as I see my palms have turned black again. The colors flipped!

CHAPTER 5

This is getting weird. Really weird. I focus again. *Pinch.* Red. *Pinch.* Black. *Pinch.* Red. *Pinch.* Black. The colors in my hands keep changing, and I keep getting pinched!

What parallel universe am I in? I need to know why this is happening. Wait. I try again. The pinch happens first, then the color changes. Now that I think about it, the colors are the same as the magnets that I had in school.

Hold on. Magnets! I stuck to the fridge like a magnet. And the monkey bars are made of metal, a metal that magnets stick to. And in class I stuck to a GIANT MAGNET.

In science, Ms. L used a big word. Pharaoh-magnetic or something. Pharaoh-magnetic sounds like the ancient Egyptian rulers were magnetic. *HAHAHA!* Magnetic pharaohs would be awesome! But that can't be it.

I think she actually said, "Ferromagnetic means metals that are attracted to magnets."

If I have magnets in my hands, I will stick to ferromagnetic metals!

Which means . . . I keep getting stuck to things that are metal because I have magnets in my hands! *HAHAHAHA!* That sounds so ridiculous!

But, if I actually have magnets in my hands, I'll be able to stick to other magnetic things. Time to put my hypothesis to the test.

I glance around looking for what I could get stuck to next. Wait, the fridge has magnets. I can use one of those. I charge upstairs to the fridge.

I reach for the "Hang in There" magnet. It is one of those flat, round ones. My mom said she bought it when I was little. Again, I don't know why she needs encouragement when she has me.

I stop myself just in time. *How am I going to get a magnet off the fridge without getting stuck to the fridge?* It's my first true challenge as Pharaoh-magnetic Boy! Because I'm the ruler of magnets!! I know the name isn't great. I'll work on it later.

"Mom! Will you grab a magnet off the fridge for me?" I shout down the hall.

"You're already in the kitchen. Why can't you grab one?" asks Mom.

I sigh. Alright, I need to get this magnet off without using my hands. I lift my leg up as high as it will go, but the magnet is slightly out of my reach.

Next, I try my elbows. I slide it down and over, but my artwork and papers on the fridge get in the way. The only option, it seems, is to use my hands. At least I know I can slide my hands off the fridge.

I slowly reach my hand toward the fridge. I wonder how close I can get before my hands are pulled to the fridge. I take a step forward and . . . my hand flies backward. It was like punching a trampoline.

I try my other hand. Same result! I stare at my hands. Why is this happening? Ten minutes ago, I was stuck to the fridge with both hands. Now, an invisible force is pushing my hands away.

I charge the fridge with both hands stretched forward. MISTAKE! My arms hit a force field and are thrown to the side.

THUMP! WOOSH! BANG!!

My head crashes into the fridge handle.

Mom to comes running. "What is going on?!"

I stand there holding my head.

"What happened?" she asks again.

"My attempt to grab the magnet was unsuccessful," I groan.

She plucks the magnet from the fridge. "Next time tell me you need help before running headfirst into the fridge. Deal?"

I crack a smile. That sounds so funny. "Deal," I say.

She sets the magnet down on the counter and starts to gather ingredients to make supper. I glare at the magnet. *How am I going to get you downstairs?* I put one hand over the other and clap them down over the magnet. I wait.

I start to feel some pressure pushing up on my bottom hand. I get down real close with my face and lift my hands to peek at what's happening. Another mistake! You'd think I would have learned by now.

The magnet flies from my hand. I close my eyes and jerk my head up just in time. The magnet slides off the counter, smacking my chest, and soars across the floor. I follow it. It ends up resting against one of our kitchen chairs' legs. Thankfully, the chair is made of wood.

Mom's phone rings. She picks up and walks to the other room.

I strategically approach the magnet on my knees. I put one hand on either side of the chair leg and clap my hands around it. I carefully slide my hands off, keeping them pushed together so the magnet cannot escape again. Once I have the magnet between my hands, I run downstairs.

CHAPTER 6

My head is still pounding from the fridge, but I am victorious! I brought a magnet downstairs!! Okay, saying it like that doesn't sound like that much of an accomplishment.

After a short celebration in the form of a dance party ... dance, dance, dance, *pinch,* dance, dance ... I get back to the magnet.

My hands are still clasped together with the magnet between. I don't want a repeat of the kitchen counter attack where the magnet flew at me.

I decide the best course of action is to drop the magnet onto the carpet in front of me. I widen my stance, straighten my arms in front of me, and pull my hands apart as fast as I can.

Nothing falls. *Did I miss it?* I look around. The carpet is white, and my magnet is black. I should be able to see it, but I don't.

I feel a sharp jolt of pain above my eyebrow. All this absurdity is giving me a headache. The headbutt to the fridge isn't helping either.

I put a hand to my head to rub it, but instead, I am slapped in the face by a magnet. *AHHH!!*

The magnet is stuck to my left hand. I stare down the magnet with my death glare. Alright, you evil piece of metal. I *WILL* get you off my hand.

I spend the next few minutes tugging, pulling, biting, smacking, flapping, scraping, falling, spinning, thrashing, screaming—

"Is everything okay down there?"

I freeze. "Yeah! I'm just . . . playing with my magnet," I shout up the stairs.

"Make sure you finish your homework."

"Ugh! Okay," I shout back. I hate homework almost as much as I hate Isaac.

Mom continues, "The school called saying you had another argument with Isaac. We'll talk about that later."

That will be our third conversation this week. *Sigh.* I wait until I hear her walk away. I need another idea to get the magnet off because nothing is working. I start to think. Facts I know:

1. I got stuck to the monkey bars.
2. I got stuck to the fridge.

3. I feel a pinch in my hands each time the color changes.
4. Now the fridge has a force field.
5. The fridge hates me.
6. I have a magnet stuck to my hand.
7. I have magnets *in* my hands?

Wait. *I have magnets in my hands.* That means I can use the other hand to get my magnet off!

I clap my hands together and pull them apart. Clap. Clap. Clap. Clap. I sound like a robot giving a round of applause. *Sigh.* It doesn't work. *What now?*

I need a break. My mind has been working in overdrive. I grab my controller and turn on my gaming system. Thankfully, the controller is mostly plastic.

I hear Mom on the phone again, and a little later she answers the door. I can't hear who she's talking to, so I focus back on my game.

"Koen, come up here. Your friend is here to see you."

Emily? What is she doing here? I run upstairs.

I sprint to the door, but Emily's not there. Instead, I come face-to-face with my enemy standing on my front step. My eyes narrow. I glance at Mom, and she gives me a thumbs up with a big smile. *Does she not remember what Isaac did? Is this her way of making us try to be friends?*

"What are you doing here?" I ask as my mom walks down the hall.

"Hi, Koen . . . Is Emily here?"

"No. Why are *you* here, Isaac? Did you come to laugh at me some more or call me mean names?"

"That's not why I came. I wanted to ask if you want to do some tricks on the monkey bars or maybe play some video games?"

Is he serious? We haven't hung out since summer, and he was so rude at recess today. He hasn't even apologized!

"I don't think so. We don't like each other, remember? That's why you're so mean to me all the time," I say as I reach for the door. My hand snaps onto the door handle. *Oh no! Not in front of Isaac!*

"It's not that I don't like you . . . It's because you chose Emily—"

"You have to go!"

His face falls, but I can't think about that. *How am I going to get my hand off?* I try to tug it off the door with small movements. My hand is hidden behind the door, but Isaac sees my arm.

His eyes narrow. "Why are you moving your arm like that?"

He is going to figure out I'm stuck to the door. I can't let him figure it out! He will start calling me a freak and tell everyone at school. Pinch!

The door slams shut in Isaac's shocked face.

Pinch! My eyes go wide. I can't believe I just slammed the door in his face. *Did he see the door close by itself?*

I peer through the small window as Isaac walks toward his mom's car. I can't tell if he knows. I take a step back and step on the "Hang in There" magnet. When did this fall off my hand?

I bend down and cup my hands over it, so it doesn't fly across the room from the force of my magnets. *Snap!* I flip my hands to see the magnet back in the center of my red palm. Not again! I drop my head into my hands. Magnet face slap! *OW!*

CHAPTER 7

Beep. Beep! BEEP! I smack the off button on my alarm clock. I run to get ready. I give myself just enough time to eat breakfast and get dressed in the morning without being late to school. That way, I can sleep for as long as possible.

"Remember to wash your face! Yesterday you went to school with a peanut butter mustache," Mom says.

I had forgotten about that. Another one of my embarrassing moments that Isaac had gleefully pointed out to his friends.

"Thanks, Mom!"

I run into the bathroom, cup my hands under the water, and bring them up to splash my face. In addition to soaking my face with water, I also smack myself with the magnet. AGAIN! *AHHHH!* I can't believe I forgot about it! *What am I going to do?*

"We need to leave right now, Koen, or you will be late!"

I run to the door without a plan. I can't get the magnet off, so I need something to hide it.

As I put on a shoe, I notice one of my gloves half-hidden behind another pair of shoes. I quickly pull on my other shoe and slide the glove on as I run to the car.

I make it through most of the day without any problems. I keep my gloved hand hidden in my lap. I'm right-handed, so it is pretty easy to get away with it. For those times when my classmates do notice, I say, "My hand is really cold."

They laugh a little then go back to doing whatever they were doing. They are used to me doing odd things.

The only one that really cares is Isaac. He hasn't said anything about yesterday, but I know he's mad. He glared at me all morning, which should be impossible because he sits three rows ahead of me, but he found a way every time Ms. L's back was turned.

Isaac spotted my glove when I sat down at the lunch table and smirked.

"You're so weird! You are only wearing one glove, and that looks stupid!" He starts a chant, "Koen looks stupid! Koen looks stupid!"

I'm sure you agree, this is a *brilliant* chant. I look around the lunch table. Emily is sitting beside me like she normally does, eating her French toast sticks and glaring at Isaac.

Everyone else stares at me waiting to see what is going to happen. No one else joins in, but Isaac's friends grin which encourage him.

"Koen looks stupid! Koen looks stupid!"

"Stop it, Isaac," Emily whispers.

I look over to her.

"Koen looks stupid!"

"Stop it, Isaac! You're being mean!!" Emily shouts at him.

My mouth drops to the floor. She never yells. I mean *ever*. She hardly speaks to anyone other than me or Sarai (her other friend). Even this summer when Isaac,

Emily, and I hung out, she was quiet around him.

I look over at Isaac, and he has this weird look on his face. I can't tell what he's thinking. We are saved by the bell, literally. Everyone at our table rushes to throw away their trash, and I run to catch up to Emily.

"Thanks for telling him to stop."

She smiles at me and whispers, "I couldn't stand it anymore! He makes me so mad when he is mean to others. Who even cares that you have a glove on?"

I quickly glance at my hand then back at her.

"Why do you have it on?"

"Uh—"

Before I could tell her, Isaac runs into us, pushing his way through. As he passes, he grabs Emily's water bottle and keeps running.

"Hey!" I shout.

I take off after him. Catching up to him is easy. He bulldozes a path through the kids in the hallway, and I just need to follow.

I reach for the water bottle. *If I could just grab it . . .* A force yanks it out of his hands into mine. The bottle suctions to the center of my hand. *Oh!* It must be metal.

He turns and tries to take it back. It is pointless. It's not like I am stronger than Isaac, but he is no match for the magnetic force between my hand and the water bottle.

He wraps both hands around the top of the bottle and tugs with all his might. One point for Magnet Boy! (I'm still working on the name).

I smile. This might be fun. I swing my arms to the right. As he starts to pull harder to the left, I whip my hands left and continue to spin. He loses his grip on the bottle and goes flying! *HAHAHAHAHA!!* I hold the water bottle above my head triumphantly.

"Koen."

Oh no. I turn and see Ms. L standing with her hands on her hips. I'm definitely getting another note home. I sigh. Still holding on to the water bottle with my right hand, I walk over to her.

The other kids pass us whispering to each other as they go up the stairs to our classroom.

"What happened?" she asks in a tone that says no funny business.

"Well, he stole Emily's water bottle, so I got it back for her!"

"I saw you throw him to the ground. How else would he end up over there on the floor?"

She makes me sound like a gladiator. I look over at Isaac laying on the floor. He stands up brushing dust off his clothes. Serves him right! I try *REALLY* hard to keep my face from showing what I feel inside, which is *HAHAHAHAHAHAHA!!* But I'm not a good actor.

"HAHAHAHAHAHAHAHAHAHAHA!!"

"Koen. That is very rude. I'm going to have to call your mom." She walks over to Isaac to check if he is alright.

He's fine. She tells us that we will both have to stay in for recess tomorrow. Right now, I don't care. I'm glad Isaac got what he deserved.

CHAPTER 8

I usually don't look forward to any class, but today I can't wait for science to get started. I might learn how to get my magnet off!

I walk into the classroom, sit down at my desk, and try to set Emily's water bottle down. As you probably already guessed, that fails. It stays glued to my hand.

I now have a fridge magnet stuck to one hand and a water bottle stuck to the other. *Sigh. What am I going to do?*

I can see Emily motioning for me to come to her table for group work. Reluctantly, I get up.

She smiles at me. "Thanks," she whispers. She reaches out for me to hand the water bottle to her.

I press my lips together. "Um, Emily, I can't give it to you right now."

Her eyebrows knit together. That's her way of saying, "What do you mean? I'm confused."

"I mean, I can't give you your water bottle." I take a deep breath. "It's kind of stuck to my hand."

She smiles again and keeps her hand out.

I give her a look to show that I am serious. "I'm telling you the truth. The water bottle will not come off." I open my hand and shake it a few times to prove it.

"Why?"

"Don't laugh, okay?" She nods. I lower my voice and lean closer to her, so my classmates will not hear. "I think I have magnets in my hands."

I can see her trying hard not to smile.

With a big breath, she whispers back, "No way, you must have something sticky on your hand, like syrup from lunch. Wash it off in the bathroom."

Ms. L begins class. Emily motions for her water bottle. I give her a *"What can I do?"* look and keep the hand holding the water bottle on my desk.

I try my best to pay attention, but I can't. I finally told someone about the magnets in my hands . . . but if Emily doesn't believe me, who will?

"You're right Dagny."

I snap out of my thoughts.

"The magnets push apart because the same poles are facing each other, like a positive and positive. When you put two of the same charges (- - or + +) together, the magnets will repel. This happens because of the energy within the magnetic field. Who can remind me what a magnetic field is?"

Hands shoot up across the classroom.

"The magnetic field is like a force field around the magnet," Mareesa starts to explain. "Depending on which side of the magnet is closer to a magnetic object, it will either pull it closer or push it away."

"Yes!" Ms. L says enthusiastically.

Do I have geniuses in my class? I don't remember learning about this stuff at all.

John adds, "If a positive pole is close enough to a negative pole, the magnets will attract each other."

Wait. *Is that what happened with my magnet and the door at home? And Emily's water bottle? Is that why they are stuck to my hands right now?*

My hand magnets are red, which are the negative poles they are talking about. That means the water bottle and fridge magnet must have positive poles, which is why they are stuck to my hands right now!

Huh. If that is the case, why didn't my hands attract or repel each other when I was clapping like a robot yesterday?

I raise my hand. "Ms. L!"

She looks at my hand. "Koen, do you need to fill up your water bottle?"

I glance up. I completely forgot I had the water bottle stuck to the hand I raised. That's embarrassing. I quickly lower it.

"No, I had a question. If you have two *really* strong magnets that are stuck together with the opposite poles, how do you get them apart?"

"You need enough energy to break the bond between them. That energy can come from you! You can pull them apart."

As if I haven't tried that. Looks like I'll need to find a different way on my own.

CHAPTER 9

At recess, I avoid the monkey bars. I walk around the backside of the playground and sit behind the big tree. Yes, it is the same one that I climbed, got stuck in, and was rescued from. Normally people don't come back here, so I will have some privacy.

I sit down and put one foot on either side of the water bottle attached to my hand. One last try. I push my legs forward with all my might. *AHHHHH!* The water bottle doesn't leave my hand, but my arm feels like it might leave my body!

"What are you doing?"

I look up to see Emily peering around the tree. I forgot Emily usually sits with Sarai back here. It is one of the only places at school she feels comfortable to talk because there are no adults around. Teachers have to stay near the foursquare court to break up arguments, usually caused by Isaac and his goons.

"Is Sarai with you?" I ask.

"No, she is with Thea and Lexi today. What are you doing?"

There is no use making up a lie. Plus, I already told her about the magnets. "I am trying to get your water bottle off my hand."

Emily comes and sits next to me. "You aren't kidding, are you?"

"No," I say, crossing my heart with my gloved hand.

She sits silently for what feels like ten minutes. "Okay. How can I help?"

I tell her about what happened in science class, at recess, and at home. I watch her face as I tell her everything. She seems to be taking this seriously, though she laughs when I tell her about smacking my head into the fridge.

"And I think your water bottle is stuck to me because it is a metal with a positive charge. I reached for it when the magnet in my hand was red. That's a negative charge. Positive and negative charges attract, which explains why the water bottle looked like it was ripped out of Isaac's hand and flew into mine."

Snap!

"What was that?" I ask as I look around. Emily shrugs her shoulders.

I jump up to check behind the tree. I get to the other side in time to see someone in a red shirt sprinting away.

"Emily, we have to find a way to get your water bottle and my fridge magnet off me! I think Isaac just heard everything!!"

She comes around the tree. "Do you remember this summer when we were hanging out?"

"Yeah, he was so mean! He would tell me my monkey bar tricks are awful and laugh at me."

"But did he ever tell anyone else or have any friends with him?"

"No, I don't think so . . . But he could tell his friends now! You never know what Isaac is going to do!!"

The bell rings for the end of recess.

Emily turns to me. "Don't worry. I have an idea how to get the water bottle off. We can figure out if Isaac knows after."

CHAPTER 10

Emily never got a chance to tell me what her idea was. I'll have to wait until after school. *Ugh.* I keep looking at the clock during math class.

This class is taking soooooooooo long, and it has only been five minutes! How will I get through an hour?!

Ms. L puts a problem on the board and gives us ten minutes to work on it. Normally, I can figure out these math problems before the time is up, but I haven't had a water bottle stuck on the hand

I write with before! This is going to be tough. At least I can move my fingers! I tip the water bottle and lower my hand to grab the marker with my fingers.

CLANG!

The water bottle smashes into the table. *Oops!* My classmates look at me. I wait for a second until they turn back around. *I've got it this time.*

I try again. The water bottle hits the marker and sends it flying off the table. It stops rolling under Sarai's table. Instead of walking, I crawl across the floor. Bad idea!

Thud. Pat. Thud. Pat. Thud. Pat.

The whole class, even Ms. L, stops to listen to the sound of the water bottle and my gloved hand against the floor. I hear some snickers from Isaac's table. At least the carpet made it a little quieter . . .

Once I get back to my table, I decide it is best to write with my left hand. I solve the math problem. I wave Ms. L over to come look at my work. Sometimes, she picks kids to share their work on the projector with the class. She stands beside me.

"Koen, I see you have the correct answer, but I can't read your work. Can you tell me what you did?"

I look at my work. *Whoa.* She's right. It looks like a kindergartener just learning how to write. I try to explain what I did, but it's hard because I can't really read my writing. I stare at my paper really hard.

"I think that might be a plus sign . . . or divide."

"I'll come back in a few minutes to see if you remember what you did," Ms. L says as she walks over to another table. But at the end of class, she picks Isaac to share his work with the class. *Ugh.*

The final bell rings, and I run outside to my mom's car. "Mom! Can Emily come over today?"

"Sure, if it is okay with her parents."

"Yes! I'll let her know." I look around and see Emily standing by her mom. Emily sees me and gives me a thumbs up. I give her a double thumbs up. Well, the best I can with a water bottle stuck to one hand. Mom smiles as Emily gets in.

"Hi, Emily."

Emily smiles back.

The ride seems like it takes forever even though I only live a few minutes away. Once we *finally* pull up to the driveway, I grab my backpack and prepare to jump out. Emily and I run to the back yard.

"I'll be in the kitchen if you need anything," Mom shouts after us.

I can't wait any longer. "What's your idea?" I ask while pulling off my glove with my teeth. What? It's not like I can use my other hand. There is a water bottle stuck to it!

"Do you remember when you were talking about what happened on the monkey bars? When you thought about letting go?"

"Yes . . ." I say, not seeing how that has anything to do with me now.

"Well, you thought really, really hard about it. Then it happened. Maybe you haven't thought hard enough about getting them off your hands yet."

I laugh. "I have! I've wanted them off my hands for hours."

"I know you want them off, but do your hands know that?"

I stare at her. Does she want me to talk to my hands? *HAHAHAHA!*

"Seriously, Koen. Think about letting go. And tell your hands to do it."

I shrug. What could it hurt? I plant my feet and stretch my arms in front of me. I stare at the back of my hands. *Let go. Get off me. Come on, do it!*

"I can't hear you!"

I squeeze my eyes shut. I want this water bottle and magnet off so bad. I need my hands back! "GET OFF OF ME!!" I shout. I feel pressure in my hands. Then a pinch. Then nothing. I open my eyes.

CHAPTER 11

"Yes! It worked!!" Emily is dancing around.

She looks a little silly, but I join her dancing my own happy dance. When we get tired, I look around.

"Where did they end up?"

"It was amazing! You shouted, and they flew across the yard. Come on, look!"

We run to the edge of the fence. Her water bottle landed on its side with a dent in it. The refrigerator magnet is lying beside the bottle. I reach down to pick them up.

"Wait!" Emily shouts at me.

Startled, I freeze. I'm still not used to hearing her yell.

"Don't touch them! You'll have them stuck to you again!"

I can't believe I already forgot!

"Thanks," I say, "and sorry about your water bottle."

"It still works," she says as she examines the bottle. She turns the bottle on its side and holds it up for me to see.

"Most water bottles aren't magnetic, but my dad put this magnet strip on the side so it would stick to our fridge at night. I kept losing water bottles around the house and could never find them in time for school. That's another reason why I'm late sometimes," she explains as she points to the black strip.

"That's why it stuck to my hand! I thought that water bottle must be magnetic."

I glance at my hands. This time I am not surprised. My palms are black.

CHAPTER 12

I catch up to Emily. "Hey, would you throw me the 'Hang in There' magnet for a second?"

"Why? It will stick to you again."

"I don't think it will."

She tilts her head. I just smile. She tosses it to me. I cup my hands for it to land in. It looks like I am going to catch it, but instead, it hits an invisible force and bounces away. Emily stares at me.

"Check out my hands. The inside is black now. It was red before when the magnet stuck to it."

She thinks for a second. "Those are the colors of the magnets in class. No wonder you said you have magnets in your hands."

She finally gets it!

"You need to figure out how to control it, so you aren't always getting stuck to things."

I nod in agreement.

"In class, they were talking about the magnetic field. That must be what the magnet hit when it bounced away," Emily says.

"I remember them talking about the rules. Opposite charges attract and the same repel. I also remember north, south, positive, negative, red, black . . . Which color is considered north? Is north positive or negative?"

Emily turns to me. "I think we need a chart or something to help us keep that straight."

We run inside in search of markers and paper.

"At least those won't get stuck to my hands. Right?" I glance at Emily.

"Right," she says. "Magnets are only attracted to other metals. Paper and markers are not metal."

We find the supplies and get to work. I ask Emily questions, and she tells me if I'm right or not. I should definitely pay more attention in school. Emily only loses one of the markers as we make the chart, so I count that as a win.

At last, we have our finished chart:

> Red = North = Negative (−)
>
> Red hands attract/stick to magnets
>
> Attract: − +
>
> Repel: − − and + +
>
> Black = South = Positive (+)
>
> Black hands repel/push away magnets

"Hey, Emily, the magnets in my hands are both black. Why don't my hands repel each other?"

"Huh, I don't know."

CHAPTER 13

Ms. L keeps Isaac and me inside for recess today like she promised. We are supposed to be doing homework, or apologizing, or something.

I choose to glare at the back of Isaac's head. He turns around and sticks his tongue out at me. I do it back.

Then I notice that Isaac has his pencil bag sitting on his desk. At the beginning of the year, Ms. L put a magnetic strip on the back of all the pencil bags. Now, they stick to the sides of our desks. I smile. It's time to figure out what Isaac knows.

I check my hand. It's red. Perfect. I spent all last night practicing how to flip the magnets in my hands. It's way easier when there isn't anything stuck to them. Plus, there is not as much of a pinch.

I stretch my arm across my desk as far as I can. I close my eyes and imagine the pencil bag flying off his desk. I open my eyes. I can't tell if it has moved.

"Come on," I mumble as I stare at the bag.

There! It starts to slide across his desk in my direction.

"Did you say something Koen?" Ms. L asks.

"No, Ms. L!"

Still, she motions at me to come over to her desk. I'll have to walk next to Isaac's desk. Perfect. As I walk past, he tries to trip me. I glare at him.

I concentrate on getting my magnet to switch in my hand. *Pinch.* I put my hand next to his pencil bag, and it flies onto the floor. *Hehe!*

Ms. L says my name again. I face her with my back to where Isaac is sitting.

"Koen, I know . . ."

I tune her out while I focus on Isaac. I hear him put the pencil bag back on his desk. My hand pinches, already knowing what I want to do next. I concentrate on pulling the bag's magnet to my hand. I hear it start to slide.

"What the heck!" Isaac yells.

I close my hand into a ball. Ms. L stops talking to me and looks at Isaac.

"What's going on?"

"My pencil bag is moving, and I'm not touching it!"

I look at Ms. L. I can see her trying not to smile.

"Why don't you stick it to the side of your desk? Then it won't move at all."

"But I'm telling you that it *did* move by itself!"

"Hmm, that is strange," she says while looking at me.

I smirk at Isaac. "Things don't just move by themselves, Isaac. Unless it was a ghost."

Ms. L has me return to my seat. I spend the rest of recess smiling at the back of Isaac's head. When everyone else comes in from outside, Isaac stands up and walks past my desk.

"I don't think it was a ghost, you freak," he whispers. "I don't know how, but I think you had something to do with it."

"Isaac, please return to your seat. Class is starting."

I'm safe; he doesn't know! He didn't hear me at recess yesterday, but I will need to make sure I don't have any more magnet mess-ups in front of him.

CHAPTER 14

After school, Emily comes over to my house again. I'm smiley the whole way home. I can't wait to tell her what I did today. I mastered my powers! Well, for the most part. We rush to the basement.

"You won't believe it! I actually can control my magnets now!" I practically shout.

"That's awesome!! Show me how you do it."

"Behold, Magnet Kid!"

Silence from Emily.

Uh . . . "I'm still working on the name." I hold my red palms out for her to watch, and I wait for that familiar pinch.

"WOW! I could see the magnets turn in your hands. It's a little freaky, to be honest."

I grin. "That's not even the best part!"

"What do you mean?"

"I used my powers today to mess with Isaac and figured out that he didn't hear us by the tree. You should have seen his eyes. It was like they were going to fall out of his head! And Ms. L thought he was making things up!! HAHAHAHA!!"

"Koen!" Emily glares at me. "Why would you do that? It's not nice. What if Isaac did that to you?"

Why isn't Emily happy? Isaac is mean to her too.

I respond, "He is so mean to everyone. And *he* doesn't have these awesome powers, so he couldn't do it to me. And if he did, I would throw him to the ground again. LIKE. A. BOSS!"

Emily puts her hands on her hips. "That does *not* make you a boss. And these powers don't give you the right to be mean. You should find ways to help others."

I stare at her. Her eyebrows scrunch together. She places her hands on her hips and her mouth is tight. *Whoa.* She is dead serious.

She stays like that until I finally sigh and say, "Alright. I won't mess with Isaac again . . . Unless he does something mean first!"

She thinks for a moment. "Well, if it's to help someone, like when you got my water bottle back for me, I guess that's okay."

Her face goes back to a normal expression.

Relieved that the lecture is over, I say, "Let's go figure out how strong my hand magnets actually are!"

CHAPTER 15

We gather as many magnetic objects as we can find and carry them to my backyard. I should say that Emily is the one carrying the objects.

I would help, but my hands would get in the way. I make sure to tell Emily that. She frowns and then smiles. She runs over to a plastic ice cream bucket where my mom keeps her gardening tools. She sets the tools on the ground and then fills the bucket with our magnetic objects.

"Here," she says as she hands me the bucket with a smile. "Your hands won't stick to plastic. Now you don't have any excuse not to help."

Well, she got me. I carry the bucket to the end of the yard and set it down next to the huge tree. My yard is a small rectangle surrounded by a wooden fence.

"It's a good thing your fence isn't metal like mine. Otherwise, you might be stuck to it right now," Emily laughs.

I laugh as I imagine it too.

We decide that we need to do a variety of tests. Emily ties the "Hang in There" magnet to a string and then ties the string around a low-hanging tree branch.

She says that this will help me figure out how far away I can be and still make a magnet move. I take three huge steps from the magnet and turn to face it.

Pinch. I reach out my red palms. Within a second, the magnet comes flying into my hands.

"Whoa, you actually broke the string! Try moving back."

Pinch. The magnet flies back to Emily who is waiting by the tree. I didn't even have to throw it. Awesome! I count out eight steps this time. *Pinch.*

"You ready?"

She nods. I raise my hands again. The magnet swings toward me. This time, the string doesn't break. The magnet pulls the string tight and freezes in the air.

I keep my hands up while Emily grabs the magnet and tries to tug it in the opposite direction. It doesn't work. She grabs onto the magnet with both hands and swings her feet up. For a second, she is hanging in the air from the magnet.

SNAP! The string breaks. Emily falls to the ground as the magnet flies to my hands.

She jumps up.

"Wow, the magnet held me in the air! I have another idea!"

Emily runs back into the house. She comes back with my baseball glove on her hand.

"This time, I'm going to hold the magnet in the glove, and you are going to pull it toward you."

We try it. Let's just say it didn't work out very well—for Emily at least. Emily sits up brushing dirt off her face, clothes, and hair.

"New plan. The magnet will still be in the glove, but I will *not* be holding it."

"How will the magnet stay in the glove?" I ask.

Emily pulls a roll of silver duct tape from the plastic bucket.

I stare at what used to be my baseball glove. Now it looks like a weirdly shaped gray blob. I make sure my hands are red, and Emily takes a few steps back.

"Let's see what you can do!"

I take a deep breath. The glove starts to rock back and forth. It begins to flop and roll toward me. The glove hits a divot and is airborne. It flies directly into my hands.

"Yes!" Emily shouts as she starts her celebration dance. "Now send the glove back without throwing it."

She holds her hands out. *Pinch.* The taped glove flies up, arcs, and falls right into her hands.

"It doesn't seem to take much effort attracting and repelling the magnets anymore," I tell her.

Then Emily grins. "I have an idea."

CHAPTER 16

"This is ridiculous. There is no way this is going to work. How is this even supposed to work? Nope! This is not something I can do."

"Enough with your excuses! Just try it."

I stand in front of the basketball hoop in my driveway. Emily stands in front of me, hands on her hips, head held high, beaming with pride, as she surveys her work. I can't see the duct-taped glove with the "Hang in There" magnet. Emily buried it underneath a mess of duct tape around the middle of the basketball hoop pole.

I flashback to five minutes ago. I was standing where I am now and watched as she ran around the pole with the roll of duct tape. Around and around and around. I can still hear her wild laughter . . . *Shudder.*

"Koen, it's the same concept. Try to pull the glove to you. You're attracting the magnet—"

"That is excessively and ridiculously duct-taped to a basketball pole!" I interrupt.

"*Hmph.*" Emily crosses her arms. "You wanted to see how strong your powers are. This is a test to find out." She glares at me.

"Alright, alright. I'll try it, but you have to stand way back." Emily skips toward the other end of the driveway.

I take a deep breath. *I can do this. I am the Master of Magnets . . . Still not the best name, but I like the* master *part. This is not the time to be thinking about this! Alright, I can do this.*

I extend my arms in front of me. *Pinch.* I concentrate on pulling the magnet toward me.

At first, nothing happens. I close my eyes and try harder. I can feel the pull between my hands and the magnet. My fingers start to squeeze around that invisible connection. I begin to feel my arms shake. I grip tighter. With all my effort, I yank my arms to the right.

I hear the magnet rip through the duct tape on the glove and then the pole.

ZZZZ!

The magnet flies into my hand. My eyes snap open. Awesome! *Pinch.* The magnet falls to the ground. *Pinch.* I'm so ready to try that again!

"Emily! It worked!"

CREEEEAK.

Blinking upward, I see that the basketball hoop is now tipping toward me.

Oh no. I should start running, but instead, I let the world know what is happening. "I AM GOING TO *DIE!!!!!! AHHHHHHHHHHHHH—*"

UMPH!

Emily charges into me, pushing me out of the way. I smack into the garage door and slide down. Emily hits the ground beside me.

"Wh—" I start.

"Look!"

The hoop continues its slow-motion fall toward where I stood . . . and toward my mom's car.

"THE HOOP IS FALLING TOWARD THE CAR!!!"

"DO SOMETHING!"

"LIKE WHAT?!?!"

"USE YOUR HANDS!!"

"MY HANDS?! I CAN'T CATCH A FALLING BASKETBALL HOOP. IT IS HEAVIER THAN IT LOOKS! IT WILL CRUSH ME!!"

Emily grabs my hand and jabs my palms where the red circle of the magnet is. *Oh!* I scramble to my feet and throw my hands out in front of me.

SQUEAK. CRUNCH. CREEEEEEAK!

"STOP! YOU'RE TURNING THE HOOP TOWARD YOU!"

That is exactly what is happening. I am still attracting the hoop, even though I am not in front of it anymore. I stand off to the right of where Emily tackled me against the garage door.

Rotating the hoop loosened the cement around it, allowing the hoop to fall much faster. Now it's facing me again, and I am in danger of the hoop toppling and crushing me into the ground. AGAIN! Emily too!

I stare straight up. The backboard is above us blocking out the sky. Dust rains down on us. I shut my eyes. No. NO. NO!!

"STOP!!" I scream.

"Koen, look at what you are doing!"

I open my eyes. The basketball hoop hasn't fallen. The magnetic force between my hands and the hoop holds it at a diagonal right above us. Dust floats to the ground around us as time stands still.

CHAPTER 17

I stare at the hoop. "Emily, what are we going to do now? I don't know how long I can hold it here."

She runs in front of my still outstretched arms.

"What are you doing?! Get out of the way!"

"Oh please. If your magnets are strong enough to pull a basketball hoop out of the ground, a person in the way will not affect them. Plus, someone needs to figure out how you got the hoop to stop. Koen, why didn't you tell me you could change one of your magnets?"

"What are you talking about? I can't. They both change."

"Not anymore." Emily touches my left hand. "This one is black and this one," she says touching my right hand, "is red."

"That must be what is keeping the hoop from falling on us."

"Yes," Emily continues, "The charges must balance each other out. One hand attracts and the other repels. If we are right, then you need to use less attraction and repel more."

"That's like when I burp and fart at the same time! Mom always says that repels anyone nearby. She calls it a 'furp.' Get it? A fart and a burp!"

Emily makes a yuck face. "'Always?' You've done that more than once? In front of your mom? Gross!"

"Are you ready for the 'furp?'"

"NO! Do *NOT* do that. You need to use more of the black magnet to repel and less of the red."

"I think I can do that. Move out of the way in case the hoop falls."

Emily runs out of the hoop's crushing zone. I start to close my fingers into my right palm to block the red magnet. *Oof.*

My left arm bends under the weight transfer. I become more aware of the invisible connection between my hand and the pole's magnet. As I start to push against that connection by straightening my arm, I hear a groan as the hoop begins to right itself.

". . . TOO FAST!"

I barely hear Emily in time. I was so focused that the black magnet repelled the basketball hoop too far. The hoop tips backward.

My right hand snaps open freezing the hoop in place. I need to use both hands if I'm going to get the hoop upright. Keeping both hands open in front of me, I take turns pulling and pushing my arms. As I straighten one arm, my other arm bends.

I do that move over and over again. I look like a glitching robot. The basketball hoop slowly rises back to its original position. I hold both arms out evenly to balance the magnetic forces.

"What now?" I ask Emily, "Will the basketball hoop stay up if I put my hands down?"

"I'm not sure. Let me try to pack in dirt around the base before you stop."

I keep my hands out while Emily runs around the hoop scooping my mom's gardening dirt around the base and stomping it in. Once she finishes, I slowly close my hands. Nothing happens. I lower my hands to my sides. Still nothing.

Emily and I glance at each other, and we burst out laughing.

"I can't believe it stayed up! Nice job, Koen!"

"That was AMAZING! I feel like I can do anything!!"

"I can't believe we were so close to being smashed by a basketball hoop! I really did not think that through. It came so close to hitting your house," Emily says.

We walk over to the front door. Emily pulls the door open. *Caw.* I glance back. A large black bird soars toward the hoop, landing on the rim. The hoop sways to the front and settles. I sigh. That could have been bad.

"Hey! What were you guys doing?" Isaac calls from the sidewalk.

"Isaac? What are you doing here?"

"You didn't answer my question."

Caw. Caw. Three more birds land on top of the basketball hoop.

CREAK!

The basketball hoop tips to the side, and the birds take flight. Before I can even take a step, the hoop falls.

Isaac dives into my neighbor's yard.

BOOM!!

The windows rattle, and the door swings closed.

"KOEN! EMILY!?" Mom comes running out of the house. She sees the fallen basketball hoop and Isaac. Her eyes get wide. "Are you all okay?"

"Yeah, we're fine. We were right by the door when it happened, and Isaac jumped out of the way."

She looks us all over anyway. "I can't believe it fell. It's been there for years."

"Yeah, that is strange," I say, trying not to sound suspicious.

Isaac glares at me. "Is it though?" he mutters under his breath. "You're lucky your mom is around. Otherwise, I'd be getting answers."

CHAPTER 18

On Monday, Emily finds me sitting behind the tree before school. "Your magnets are so strong that you can pull a basketball hoop out of the ground. That is so AWESOME!"

I shush her. "Not so loud, or someone will hear you!"

"Shouldn't you be telling people? Why do you want to keep your powers a secret?"

"I feel like it would draw all this attention that I don't want, especially from him." I nod my head toward where Isaac is *barely* winning at foursquare. Okay . . . he's actually dominating.

Emily nods her head in understanding. She whispers, "We should try something bigger than a basketball hoop to see if you can control that too."

"Like what?"

"I'm not—"

I glance around to see why Emily stopped talking and find Isaac standing behind me. *Great.* I jump to my feet.

"What do *you* want, Isaac?"

"I'm so much better than everyone in our class at foursquare, so I got bored. I thought it would be fun to destroy you on the monkey bars. You know, make sure *all* the *losers* know who rules recess. Plus, if you get stuck, maybe the firetruck will come rescue you again," he smirks.

My eyes narrow and my heart beats faster at his challenge. I could take him any day and win . . . except, maybe I can't. Not with these magnets in my hands.

The last thing I need is to be thrown from the monkey bars by my magnets. My classmates would laugh at me for days. Or worse, I might end up tearing the monkey bars out of the ground like the basketball hoop. They would hate me then.

But I can't let Isaac just think he won. He will never let it go, and I've never backed down from his challenges before. That will definitely make him more suspicious.

"Please, you *wish* you were half as awesome as I am. I've already proven I'm the best on the monkey bars *soooooo* many times. Instead, why don't you try to be more original with your 'challenges,'" I say as I put air quotes around the word challenges.

Isaac clenches his teeth, and his face gets red, so red that he starts to look like a tomato. *HAHA!* Serves him right for calling me a loser.

"Can't think of anything?" I taunt, "I guess original thinking isn't something *you* rule at."

His eyes almost bulge out of his head. With a shout, he charges at me. *Oops!* I turn and sprint away from the tree. As I run for my life, I realize I only have two options: run to the blacktop by the foursquare court that leaves nothing between me and Isaac or run through the playground where there are several obstacles so he can't easily charge me. Playground it is!

I pound up the steps careful to keep my hands closed, so I don't touch the metal railings, poles, or ladders . . . this might have been a mistake. But it's too late to run to the blacktop because Isaac is right behind me. I throw myself down the plastic tunnel slide crossing my fingers that Isaac doesn't switch directions and catch me at the bottom.

He's smart though and does just that. He grabs my leg and yanks me off the slide. My back hits the woodchips with a thud. *OOF!*

I scramble to free myself and stand up, kicking his stomach in the process. He stumbles back a few steps, but that doesn't stop him.

Back on my feet, I sprint in the opposite direction, toward the swings. I glance behind me. *Oh no, oh no, oh no!* He's still coming after me, and I'm running toward metal chains. Wait! I can use the chains to protect myself.

I sprint through the swings and turn back toward Isaac. Surprise flashes on his face, but then he grins and charges straight at me.

I throw my hands up. The swings fly at Isaac smacking him onto the ground. I drop my arms quickly, and the swings fall too.

His eyes widen, but he stands up to try again. He runs at an angle this time. I throw my hands up. The swings miss and fly right next to him as he runs through the middle.

I pull my hands to the side and back toward me. For a second, it looks like both swings will miss him, but one catches his back from behind and sling shots him through the air, past me, where he slides through the woodchips.

He lays there stunned for one second, two, three . . . I start to get a little worried that maybe I really hurt him. Then, he sits up, woodchips sticking out of his hair.

"Both of you to the principal's office. Now!" Ms. L yells as kids start to crowd around us whispering and pointing.

I've never seen her angry before. It's kind of scary. I start to tell her that none of this is my fault, but she cuts me off.

"Your parents will be meeting with me today. You both have gone too far."

CHAPTER 19

My mom does not look happy as she walks out of the classroom with Isaac's parents right behind her. Mom runs to the bathroom while Isaac's parents talk to him.

They whisper quiet enough that I can't hear what they say, but I know he's not happy about it because he glares at me like he wants to yank me off a slide again as they walk around the corner.

As I wait for my mom to return, Ms. L walks into the hall.

"Koen, I thought we discussed this during detention last week."

"I know. You want me to be nice to Isaac, but he was going to kill me! Didn't you see him pull me off the slide?!"

"You should be nice to Isaac, but that's not what I'm talking about, Koen. You should take my advice."

What is she talking about? "*Uh*, what advice?"

She tilts her head, her eyebrows knitting together.

Why is she confused? She's the one not making sense.

"It's time to go, Koen," my mom says as she walks toward us. "Oh Ms. L, I just want to apologize again for Koen's actions the last few weeks at school. I know he and Isaac don't get along anymore, but I'm not sure what's gotten into him," she looks at me and shakes her head.

My face falls, "Mom, it's not just me! Isaac did so much stuff too!"

"We can talk about this when we get home."

She is silent the whole way home while I try to figure out how to tell her about all the unbelievable stuff that's happened to me over the last few days without her thinking it's my "overactive imagination" or me just trying to prove I'm better than Isaac.

I have definitely been in these situations before. I mean, I haven't had to run for my life and fight off Isaac, but I've had to explain the situations I get myself into.

Remember the tree I was rescued from? Isaac told the whole class that I couldn't climb trees, and that he saw me cry like a baby because I'm afraid of heights. I couldn't let the whole class believe that was true.

I only *looked* like I was crying one time on the monkey bars because I was swinging upside down and a woodchip fell in my eye. Whose eyes wouldn't water at that?!

So, I climbed the tree to prove to everyone that I could, and that Isaac is a liar. It worked until I couldn't get down. The tree is huge! I had to jump from the bars on playground to reach the lowest branch, but I couldn't get down the same way. I also wasn't about to jump down and splat on the ground in front of everyone.

It backfired, and my classmates all believed Isaac was right. Their laughter is what brought Ms. L over to figure out what was going on.

Sigh. My mom was disappointed then too. She told me that I didn't have to prove myself to anyone, especially someone who is mean. Accepting his challenges gives him the power.

She also thought I should try to talk with Isaac to figure out why he became an evil villain with the life purpose of making mine miserable. (Not her words exactly, but close enough.)

What will my mom think if I tell her that I have magnets in my hands? If she believes me, then she'll know I was responsible for the basketball hoop falling. What if she makes me pay to get it fixed?

That's what she did when I got too excited about Christmas presents one year. I didn't read who the presents were for and shook a present meant for my aunt so hard the fancy, little glass jars broke. (Mom called them an Egyptian perfume bottles.)

After paying for those, I couldn't afford the new video game that came out a few weeks later. I can't afford to pay for a basketball hoop. I'll be paying Mom back until I'm forty!

So, I can't tell her about my magnets. But how do I explain what happened today?

CHAPTER 20

I find Emily the next morning.

"What happened?" she asks.

"My mom is so mad. Once she found out Isaac and I were challenging each other to figure out who was the best, she grounded me saying that I should know by now not to fight with him."

"Does she know about the magnets?"

"No. I want to keep it that way, so I don't have to spend every dime I have fixing the basketball hoop. Not playing video games for a week is bad enough."

Emily laughs, "Would she really make you pay for it?"

"I don't want to find out!"

The bell rings, and we run to the doors with everyone else. As we walk up the stairs, I hear a voice behind me.

"I figured it out, and I know you're behind it . . . I know what you can do."

Fear surges through me. I whip around and come face-to-face with Isaac.

"You think you can get me in trouble with Ms. L and my parents, act like I'm stupid about the whole basketball hoop incident, and then fight me with swings? I'll make sure you regret it."

Emily tugs on my arm to continue up the stairs. I start to follow.

Faking confidence, I turn my head so Isaac can hear me, "I don't know what you are talking about. Plus, after that throw down in the hallway last week *and* with the swings, I'm surprised you would want a rematch so soon."

Red splotches form on Isaac's cheeks and neck. I keep myself from running up the stairs, hoping that he won't do anything in front of so many people. But he tried to kill me yesterday on the playground, so I don't have much hope.

Ms. L waits by the door giving us our morning high fives. I stick my hand up as I rush by. I start putting my backpack in my locker.

How did he figure out that I have magnets in my hands? Does he actually know?

"Hey, Koen, catch!"

I look over my shoulder to see Isaac throw something small in my direction. I whirl around. Without thinking, I raise my hands. The object halts in mid-air.

Emily stares at me with wide eyes. Her eyes start to dart between the object and me. *Oh crap!* Isaac's friends stare at it. I drop my arms and the object falls straight down.

I walk as slowly as I can toward the object. I make sure to take the long way around the desks, so I don't draw attention to myself. My classmates that noticed huddle around the object on the floor.

"What was it?" I ask.

"One of the magnets Ms. L uses to hold up papers on the board," Emily replies.

CHAPTER 21

I can't believe I froze the magnet in front of my classmates. *UGH!* What was I thinking? And now Isaac must have figured out everything! He will tell his friends the first chance he gets.

Ms. L started teaching ten minutes ago, and I haven't heard a thing. I'm not even sure what we are learning about today.

Emily pokes me and points to the class lining up.

"What's going on?"

"Are you joking? Ms. L just told us. It's time for the field trip," she whispers.

"Oh, that's today? Awesome! No school!!"

Everyone else is already in line. We rush to find our spots as the class leaves the room. Then we march down the stairs and out the door. It sounds like an army is coming.

I start patting my hands on my legs to the beat. Then I add in my own rhythm. *Pat. Pat. Pa-Pa-Pa Pat. Pa-Pat. Pa-Pa-Pa-Pa-Pa Pat.* I go faster and faster until my hands can't keep up with my brain.

"Koen! To the front with me." Ms. L says over my music.

As I walk to the front of the line, Isaac sticks out his foot. I try to jump over it, but my back leg catches on his, and I fall to the ground.

Isaac bends down like he is going to help me up and whispers, "Now you're the one who looks stupid, you magnetic weirdo. Just wait until everyone knows how messed up you actually are."

My stomach drops. *He does know!* I try not to react, so I glare at him as I stand up.

We find seats on the bus. I sit next to Ms. L in the front, Isaac sits in the back with his friends, and Emily sits behind me with Sarai. I hear Emily groan. I turn around to figure out what's wrong. *Does she know that Isaac knows?*

"My water bottle," she mouths at me.

"I'm sure we'll find it back at school. It's probably on your desk."

She shakes her head, "I had it in my hand before we got on the bus. I don't know what happened to it. I don't know how I keep losing everything," she whispers.

I start to respond, but catch my classmates looking at me. A lot of them are looking at me. I plop down and slouch further in my seat.

Ms. L turns to me like she wants to tell me something. Maybe she will finally tell me her advice, but before she speaks, John comes running to the front to tell Ms. L that Isaac and his crew are daring others to sit underneath the last bus seat and then trapping them with their legs.

It must be a *total* shock that Isaac doesn't like to be mean just to me and Emily. So, Ms. L ends up at the back of the bus.

At least that is keeping Isaac busy from telling everyone what he knows about me. Once they know, not only will I be the class screwup, but I will be renamed as the magnetic weirdo class screwup.

UGH!!! I will never live this down. It will follow me through into middle school and high school. I'm going to be a weirdo forever, and no one will really want to be friends with me. They already just hang around to see what I will mess up next. When I get home, I'm telling Mom we need to move.

When the bus finally stops, we follow Ms. L to a stairway that leads down to a large, circular platform overlooking a river. Ms. L tells us to find a spot to sit on the stairs and listen to the presenters explain what we will see on our field trip today. That sounds boring!

I watch the river instead. It's windy today, so the water splashes against the bank. I notice some rocks sticking up from the river. A little bird hops along the rocks. I nudge Emily to check out the bird.

She nudges me back pointing at the presenter.

I refocus and hear the last part of what the presenters say.

". . . is the Arc of Dreams!"

CHAPTER 22

We walk up and down a bunch of sidewalks. As we walk, we stop at lots of metal sculptures, and our tour guide talks about them. Some of them are animals. Some are people. I usually would touch them all, but I keep my hands balled at my side. I cannot risk destroying them like the basketball hoop!

We walk onto a bridge that goes across the river I was looking at earlier. The tour guide starts to talk again.

"I saved the best for last. This last sculpture is called the Arc of Dreams. Look above you. This metal sculpture bends over the river forming an arc into the clouds."

We all look up. The sculpture is huge. The sculpture starts on the left side of the bridge we are standing on. The metal twists and intertwines in a spiral that continues up into the sky. Then it curves back to touch the ground on the right side of the bridge. It's like a slide for giants.

How hard would it be to climb? I wonder, as Isaac runs into me from behind, and I stumble forward.

"I'm going to prove once and for all that I am the best by climbing to the top. I bet you can't beat me, magnetic loser."

I look at the base of the sculpture to the arc. It would be easy to beat him . . . I'm way faster than Isaac. And then he would stop talking about my powers, or at least people wouldn't believe him!

"You wish, Isaac! I could beat you anytime, anywhere!"

Emily pokes me, and I turn toward her.

"What? I'm about to beat Isaac in the most epic way EVER!"

"The arc is metal. You can't touch it!"

UGH!!!!! I can't even prove to everyone that I'm the best! How else am I going to keep him from talking?! This is RIDICULOUS!!!

I whip around to tell Isaac the race is off and maybe beg him not to tell anyone else about my magnets, but he is gone. He's already across the bridge.

Isaac wraps his hands around one of the base poles that starts the spiral. His hands can't reach around it, so he takes a few steps back and runs at it. He jumps, grabbing hold of a horizontal piece, then walks his feet up a side pole and crouches on the horizontal piece.

He continues to jump and walk his feet up until he is about halfway up the arc's side. There, he wraps his arms around a pole that is part of the spiral and inchworms up the pole.

After a minute, Isaac's progress starts to slow. That should be me! If I could climb it, I would already be at the top!

Ms. L gets the class's attention, "Only five more minutes on the bridge, then it will be time to go."

I turn back to look at Isaac. He is almost to the top of the arc.

"Ms. L, look at Isaac!"

"Where is he?" she asks looking around the bridge at the students.

"He's on the spiral!"

Ms. L's head shoots up. "Oh my! Isaac, get down from there!"

Isaac continues to inch his way along the pole. He doesn't even look down.

"Maybe he can't hear you," I tell her.

Ms. L rushes over to the tour guide. Both are on their phones within seconds. I don't know who they are calling about this, but I hope it's someone with a camera. This is *AWESOME,* even if it is Isaac.

Soon the whole class is watching Isaac. At this point, Isaac makes it to the top of the sculpture where it arcs over the bridge we are standing on. Someone starts a chant, and we all join in. Even me. It almost feels like old times when I would cheer him on during one of his tricks.

"ISAAC, ISAAC, ISAAC!"

He finally hears us. He looks down and waves.

The wind picks up. He tries to wrap his arm around the pole but can't get a grip. Everyone on the bridge holds their breath. He tries again.

This time he gets it, but his legs slip off and begin to flail. It looks like he is trying to run on air. He tries three times to swing his legs back up to the pole, but he fails. Then he stops moving his legs and just hangs there.

"HELP!!!!"

"DON'T MOVE! HELP IS COMING!" Ms. L shouts up to him.

I don't think he hears her because he continues to shout, "HELLLLLLLLLP!!!!! HELLLLLP ME!!!!!! HELLLLLLLLLP!!!!!"

Ms. L turns to me, "Koen—"

"I AM SLIPPING!!!!!"

We all gasp. If he falls, he will either land on the bridge or in the water. The rock-filled water. He will most likely die either way. Instead of keeping that opinion to myself, I let everyone know.

"HE IS GOING TO *DIE!!!!!!!!!!!!!!!!!!!!!!!!!*"

He might have heard me because he starts to kick his legs again.

Emily runs up to me whispering, "Koen, you have to do something."

"I can't do anything! I don't have wings! I can't fly!"

She cups her hands to whisper-shout in my ear, "Use your powers!"

"Emily, I can't use my powers. Everyone will see, and I don't know if it will even work. Plus, he is so mean to us."

"But you said it yourself a second ago! He is going to die if you don't!"

I don't want him to die . . . I don't hate him that much. Why does Emily have to be right about everything?

CHAPTER 23

I take a deep breath. I need to think through my options.

Option 1: I do nothing, and Isaac dies.

Option 2: I try to help Isaac, my powers don't work, and he dies, but at least I can say I tried.

Option 3: I try to help Isaac, I save him, and he is nice to me forever. Everyone at school is nice to me. I never have to wait in line for the monkey bars. I never have to do homework again. I never have to eat vegetables. I can play video games forever!

Okay, some of these won't happen, but I can hope.

"You're right Emily. I should help Isaac. Even if he is mean."

"Quick! He is going to fall!"

I look up at where he is hanging. He seems to have re-gripped the pole and is no longer slipping. He is safe for a moment. I glance around and see . . . I have a plan! I take off running.

"Where are you going? I thought you were going to help!" Emily whisper-shouts after me.

I run to the edge of the bridge. I put my hands on the base of the spiral. *SNAP!* The attraction between my hands and the metal spiral is stronger than on the monkey bars or the fridge. I dig my feet into the ground and throw my hands to the right.

POP! POP! SCREECH!

The metal spiral tears away from the base poles. *Pinch.* The spiral repels underneath to the other side, unwrapping itself. *Pinch.* The spiral unfolds over the top and straightens.

I start to hear voices all around me.

"What is he doing? How is he doing that?!"

I refocus on the spiral. I just need to have it reach Isaac. If I keep unwrapping the spiral until it reaches Isaac, I can lower the end to the grass next to me, and Isaac can slide to safety.

Only two more loops. I move to pull it over again. As it begins to unwrap, the structure starts to tip toward me. Isaac yells something, but I can't hear him over the wind.

"You have to stop moving the spiral! The sculpture is moving too much, and Isaac is going to fall!" Emily shouts.

I freeze, holding the metal in place. Was that Emily? I whip my head around to look at her.

"Emily, you're talking in front of everyone!"

Her face gets red. "To save someone's life! This is not the thing to focus on. Isaac is going to fall!!"

I look up at Isaac. I can't let him fall, but I can't pull any more of the spiral off without him falling. This is too much stress!!

"Emily, what should I do?"

"The bridge! Lower the metal that you already pulled off to the bridge. Make sure not to move the structure! I'll see if I can get Isaac to move to the slide."

Emily takes off to the center of the bridge and begins shouting at Isaac. I focus on the metal I have already pulled off the spiral. I can't pull more off, but I can fold what I have over the top of the structure and let the rest come straight down to the bridge.

When I stopped pulling the structure, my magnets changed to one red and one black. I keep them the same and drag my red hand down. The metal starts to lower. I continue pulling the metal down while using my black hand to slow its descent. This way, Isaac isn't shaken by the metal's movement.

The metal reaches the railing of the bridge. It will be a perfect slide for Isaac . . . if he can get to it. I run to see if Emily has made any progress telling Isaac what he needs to do.

"I don't think he can hear me, but he understands. He is starting to make his way toward the slide."

Isaac still can't get his legs back on the pole. He moves one arm at a time inching closer to the spiral that will get him to safety. I start to hear sirens in the distance.

Isaac must too because he starts to whip his head from side to side. The movement causes one of his arms to slip off the sculpture.

"Oh no! He is going to fall this time!" Emily shouts and covers her eyes.

I freeze. Isaac loses his grip completely and drops through the air. There is only 50 feet between him and the rocky river. Now 40. I tear my hands through the air.

SCREECH!

The top section of the metal slide rips away. My hands move right, down, and up.

The flat piece of metal moves with my hands. I stop it halfway between the water and Isaac.

If he hits it at this speed, it will feel like face planting into concrete. Does he deserve it though? The downside is that could kill him . . .

Oh idea! I push the metal up toward Isaac as fast as I can.

Isaac begins screaming, "WHAT ARE YOU DOING?! YOU'RE GOING TO KILL ME!"

I don't slow down. He starts twisting in the air. His legs and arms flail like he is trying to run away.

Right before the metal slams into him, I throw up my red hand causing the metal to stop. I pull my hands down, though not as fast as before. Isaac continues falling with the metal right beneath him. I slow the descent of the metal even more allowing Isaac's feet to touch it before pushing up slightly.

SPLAT!

Isaac belly flops onto the metal. *Oops! I must have pushed up too hard.* I use both hands to control the speed as I continue to pull the platform down, slowing the fall.

I begin to pull the metal piece toward the bridge. I can't believe how big it is. I land it next to me on top of both side railings as Isaac lies on his stomach in the middle.

"Isaac! Are you alright?" Ms. L asks.

"Ugh . . ." he moans.

"Can you move?"

"I can help Ms. L!" I say with pride.

I push on the side of the metal closer to us with my black magnet and raise my red hand to pull the other side up. The metal piece tips toward us causing Isaac to roll right off and onto the ground.

THUD!

"Ouch!"

"Sorry! I thought you would catch yourself," I explain.

"Well, I *didn't!*" Isaac jeers as he stands.

CHAPTER 24

We glare at each other for a minute. I guess my dream of Isaac being nice to me won't come true. That means the other stuff like no homework, no chores, no waiting in line for the monkey bars won't come true either! *UUUUUUUUGH!* Why did I even save him?!

Emily breaks the glaring contest by saying, "I'm glad you're okay, Isaac."

Isaac looks at his feet. "Thanks. Me too," he says as his cheeks get red.

He looks back at me. "I guess I should thank you too, Koen. You know, for actually saving me . . . Thanks." He continues, "Maybe you aren't such a weirdo. What you did was kind of cool. You were like some sort of metal master."

"Actually, I'm more of a magnet master. Hey, Emily, that should be what I call myself . . . Magnet Master!"

I turn, holding one hand on my hip and raising the other one to the sky. "I am Magnet Master!"

The world doesn't stop as it does in superhero movies. The paramedics run past me to Isaac. The bus drives up to take us home.

As I turn back, I notice Ms. L watching me. Her smile widens, and she gives me a small nod before starting to explain what happened to the paramedics.

My classmates gather around the base of the "Arc of Dreams" pointing at me and the metal slide. Well, what is left of it. After I ripped the top of it off, the rest fell into the river.

"Let's go back to the bus," Emily says. "You saved Isaac, and we've seen all the sculptures! There is nothing else to do."

"Yeah, I can't wait to get home and eat some yogurt!"

We begin walking to the bus.

As we pass Isaac's friends, Daevion shouts, "Koen, you saved him!"

My classmates begin chanting, "KOEN, KOEN, KOEN!"

No. I think in my head. *I am not just Koen anymore.*

(Cue theme song.)

I turn to face them. "Actually, you can call me . . . Magnet Master!"

CHAPTER 25

I find my seat on the bus and Emily sits down beside me, quiet again. Our classmates crowd around us.

"Koen, I can't believe you saved him!"

"How did you move the metal?!"

"The way you controlled the sculpture was so cool, and when you ripped off that piece to catch Isaac . . . AMAZING!"

I just sit there stunned. This is not the reaction I thought they would have. They've always laughed at what I do. I never expected the awe I see in their faces. Emily shifts uncomfortably in her seat.

Ms. L tells everyone to find their seats and quiet down. My classmates find their spots still discussing "Magnet Master and Koen's amazing abilities."

Before Ms. L finds her seat, she bends down and says, "I always knew you could do it. I'm glad you finally took my advice."

"You knew?!" I gasp.

Emily's eyes go wide.

"Everyone has power, Koen. But believing in yourself is the greatest power you can have. No matter how different you think you are, when you believe in yourself, you can do things no one ever thought you could. Although, manipulating metal is very unexpected," she says with a grin.

Ms. L turns and walks down the aisle, and I realize she never actually answered my question.

What a weird day. I glance at Emily. I can't believe she yelled in front of everyone today, even adults! I also can't believe I saved Isaac, even if saving a villain is a classic superhero move.

I've definitely changed since I got these magnets stuck in my hands, Emily has, and I guess Isaac has too. Maybe he isn't totally evil. I wonder if things will be different tomorrow.

"Hey, Emily, do you think we are different now?"

"Yes and no," she whispers. "We've done some incredible things I could have never imagined, but we were pretty different to begin with."

We were different. We still are.

I used to hate the thought of being labeled as different from everyone else, but I wouldn't have been able to save Isaac if I weren't. If Emily hadn't shouted in front of everyone, Isaac would have fallen. If Isaac hadn't been daring enough to climb up the arc, I wouldn't have realized that it's okay for people to know about me being Magnet Master.

Maybe being different is not such a bad thing. In fact, I'm starting to think it's pretty great.

EPILOGUE

Hey! You're still here! What did you think of my story? Pretty AMAZING, right? Now that you know how I became Magnet Master, I need to tell you that my life from that point on has been PHENOMENAL!

I mean, if you thought superstars were popular, try becoming a real-life superhero and see what that does for you. I don't really worry about embarrassing myself anymore. I could probably fall flat on my face crying and still be the most popular person ever. (Don't worry, all this popularity isn't going to my head.)

Emily still isn't a huge fan of all the attention, but I tell her if she's going to be my partner (she did *not* like it when I called her my sidekick), she's going to have to get used to it.

Also, thank you everyone who was extremely concerned about me no longer being able to dominate the monkey bars. I'm touched by your concern, but I must let you know that I figured out how to use my magnets to my advantage so I can seriously KICK BUTT on the monkey bars again with even cooler tricks! Isaac didn't stand a chance before, and there is no hope for him now!

Speaking of Isaac, I'd love to say that he changed and became a nicer person or that we are back to being best friends . . . I mean we tolerate each other now and even eat lunch together, but he gets a little prickly when new people join our group.

Oh! That reminds me, if you thought my story was AMAZING, wait until you meet—

Cough, cough, cough.

Oh, my bad! I'm not supposed to reveal their identity yet. You're not going to want to miss it though. Until next time, stay safe my friends. I can't catch everyone with a flying sheet of metal.

Magnet Master out!

ACKNOWLEDGEMENTS

To my family who has always believed in me, I would not have been able to write this book without your support. I cannot begin to express the gratitude I have for each of you.

To my brothers who were my first readers, thank you for your giggles and feedback throughout this story. You three kept my audience alive.

To my sister who meticulously proofread my story, thank you for being brutally honest. I'm sure you will continue to do so even without me asking.

To my mom who encouraged me from the moment I shared my barely formed idea to me writing my last word, thank you for being my cheerleader.

To my dad who sparked the idea that I could be an author many times throughout my life until I saw it too, thank you. You gave me feedback and shared the scientific explanations I needed to make this story balance science with fictional pizzazz.

To Jacob who unapologetically goes for what he wants, you light a fire inside me to pursue my dreams. The never-ending laugher helps too!

To Lisa Davis who has worked with me over the last year, your ideas helped shape Koen's story into one that readers will love. You are a phenomenal editor, and I am incredibly lucky to have found you.

To Basia Tran who made my design ideas come to life, you are a fantastic cover artist.

And to my reader, thank you for taking a chance on this book. I hope you enjoyed Koen's story as much as I enjoyed writing it.

Made in the USA
Monee, IL
02 May 2023

32822586R00092